This book is dedicated to
JERRY AND BULLY

Copyright © 2000 by Todd Parr

First Edition

Library of Congress Cataloging-in-Publication Data

Parr, Todd.
    Zoo do's and don'ts / Todd Parr. — 1st ed.
      p.   cm.
    Summary: Presents twelve pairs of do's and don'ts for having fun with
animals at the zoo, such as "Do take a nap with a hippo" but "Don't let
him steal the covers."
    ISBN 0-316-69212-3
    [1. Zoo animals — Fiction. 2. Zoos — Fiction.] I. Title.
    PZ7.P2447Dog   2000
    [E] — dc21   98-49137

10 9 8 7 6 5 4 3 2 1

TW

Printed in Singapore

Zoo
Do's and Don'ts

TODD PARR

Little, Brown and Company
Boston New York London

Don't

Let Him Steal all the Covers

DO

Hop Up
and Down
with a
Kangaroo

DO

Go to the Movies with a Skunk

Make her Mad

DO

Brush Your Hair with a Lion

Wash Your Clothes
with a Rhino

Don't

Hang them on his
Horns to Dry

Do

Play Games
with a Leopard

Don't

Play
Connect-the-Dots

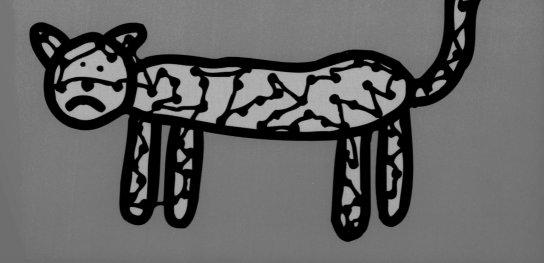

DO

Go to
the Library
with a
Snake